Row, Row, Row Your Boat

Row, Row, Row Your Boat

Pippa Goodhart

Illustrated by
Stephen Lambert

CROWN PUBLISHERS, INC. ♛ NEW YORK

Row, row, row your boat
Gently down the stream.
Merrily, merrily, merrily, merrily,
Life is but a dream.

Hoist, hoist, hoist your sail,
We're setting out to sea.
We're sailing to an island—
Georgie, you, and me.

Leap, leap, leap ashore,
Jump onto the land.
We're taking off our shoes and socks
To feel the nice hot sand.

Thump, bump, humpety-bump,
Who's that on the track?
A great big friendly elephant!
Let's climb up on his back.

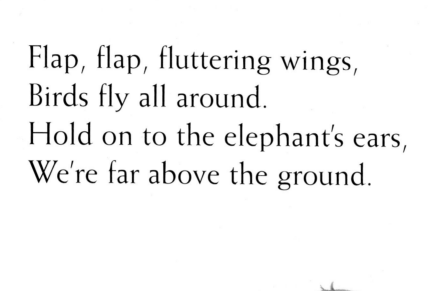

Flap, flap, fluttering wings,
Birds fly all around.
Hold on to the elephant's ears,
We're far above the ground.

Slip, slip, slip and slide
Down the elephant's nose—
To see the snakes and spiders
That live around his toes.

Up, jump, hurry along,
Clambering through the plants.
I can see the monkeys!
Let's join them in their dance.

Swing from arms, swing from tails,
Swooping through the trees.
Shaking all the flowers down
And making Georgie sneeze.
Achoo!

Push, poke, tug, and pull.
The monkeys like to tease.
They pull the tail of something big
That's hiding in the trees.

Grr, grr! What's that noise?
Oooh, it's a lion's roar!
Quick, he's chasing after us,
Let's race back to the shore.

Run, run! Find the boat
And push it out to sea.
Before the lion catches us
And has us for his tea.

Row, row, row your boat
Gently up the stream.
Merrily, merrily, merrily, merrily,
Was it just a dream?

For Hairy Mary
P. G.
To Hayley, with love
S. L.

Published by Crown Publishers, Inc., a Random House company, 201 East 50th Street,
New York, New York 10022. Published in Great Britain in 1997 by WH Books Ltd., an imprint
of Reed Consumer Books Limited, London. First American edition, 1997.

CROWN is a trademark of Crown Publishers, Inc.

http://www.randomhouse.com/

Printed in China

Library of Congress Cataloging-in-Publication Data

Goodhart, Pippa.

Row, row, row your boat / Pippa Goodhart ; illustrated by Stephen Lambert.—1st ed.
p. cm.
Summary: In this version of a familiar song, the occupants of a rowboat
have an adventure on a jungle island. Includes music.

ISBN 0-517-70970-8 (trade)

1. Children's songs. American—Texts. [1. Jungle animals—Songs and music.
2. Songs.] I. Lambert, Stephen, ill. II. Title.

  PZ8.3.G6225Ro   1997
782.42164'0268—dc21   97-7095

10 9 8 7 6 5 4 3 2 1